LOTTIE'S LETTER

Written by Gordon Snell

Illustrated by Peter Bailey

Orion Children's Books
and
Picture Dolphins

For dearest Maeve
with all my love
G.S.

Book design by Tracey Cunnell

First published in Great Britain in 1996
by Orion Children's Books
a division of the Orion Publishing Group Ltd
Orion House
5 Upper St Martin's Lane
London WC2H 9EA

A catalogue record for this book
is available from the British Library
Printed in Italy

Lottie and Max heard a sad cry from the flower-bed:
"Yeeee-ow! Yeeee-ow!"

Among the flowers, they saw a little dog. Lottie picked it up. It held out a paw.

"Look!" said Max. "There's a piece of glass in it."

Lottie held the paw gently.
She pulled the glass out,
and said: "People shouldn't
leave litter like that around.
It's cruel."
"Someone should do
something to stop it,"
said Max.

"We'll do something!"
said Lottie. "We'll write
a letter, and take it to
the Queen of the World!
People will listen if
she tells them they're
messing everything up."

"She won't take any notice of
a letter from us," said Max.
"But she will, if it's signed by
the animals too!" said Lottie.

THE WORLD IS PRECIOUS, EVERY BIT –
PLEASE DON'T MAKE A MESS OF IT!
Lottie

So they got a big
piece of paper and Lottie wrote:
THE WORLD IS PRECIOUS, EVERY BIT -
PLEASE DON'T MAKE A MESS OF IT!
She wrote her name, and Max wrote his.

Then they got the dog to put
a paw in some sticky mud,
and stamp it on the paper.

Now Lottie's letter had
a **PAW-MARK.**

They saw a pigeon with its beak stuck together with a piece of chewing-gum.

They took the chewing-gum out, and the pigeon put its claw in the mud and its mark on the paper.

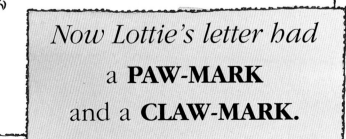

Now Lottie's letter had
a **PAW-MARK**
and a **CLAW-MARK.**

Down came a seagull with its wings covered in oil spilt in the sea.

Lottie said: "You see, it's not just litter. There's all kinds of muck messing up the world."

She got the seagull to put its wing on the letter.

Now Lottie's letter had a **PAW-MARK** a **CLAW-MARK** and a **WING-MARK.**

They heard a bee buzzing around.

Lottie said: "If the flowers all die from fumes and pollution, bees won't be able to lick them and make honey."

They got the bee to make a mark with its sting.

Now Lottie's letter had
a **PAW-MARK**
a **CLAW-MARK**
a **WING-MARK**
and a **STING-MARK.**

A frog hopped from the pond. It gulped fresh air, glad to be out of the slimy, dirty water. It put the mark of its long leg on the letter.

Now Lottie's letter had
a **PAW-MARK**
a **CLAW-MARK**
a **WING-MARK**
a **STING-MARK**
and a **LEG-MARK.**

They saw a duck sitting by the pond. It stood up,
and there underneath it was an egg.
"If the food they eat gets polluted," said Lottie,
"eggs that ducks and other creatures lay won't hatch out."
The duck rolled its egg over the letter.

Now Lottie's letter had
a **PAW-MARK**
a **CLAW-MARK**
a **WING-MARK**
a **STING-MARK**
a **LEG-MARK**
and an **EGG-MARK.**

They walked by the river and saw a salmon.
"Look!" said Lottie. "The water's all mucky."

The salmon jumped out and rolled over on the letter, leaving the pattern of its scales there.

Now Lottie's letter had

a **PAW-MARK**

a **CLAW-MARK**

a **WING-MARK**

a **STING-MARK**

a **LEG-MARK**

an **EGG-MARK**

and a **SCALE-MARK.**

They came to the seashore and saw
a dolphin jumping in the sea.
   Lottie said: "If the sea gets poisoned
by nuclear waste, the dolphins will die."

The dolphin swam to the shore,
dipped its tail in some sludgy sand,
and slapped it down on the paper.

Now Lottie's letter had
a **PAW-MARK**
a **CLAW-MARK**
a **WING-MARK**
a **STING-MARK**
a **LEG-MARK**
an **EGG-MARK**
a **SCALE-MARK**
and a **TAIL-MARK.**

"Is the letter finished?" asked Max.

"No!" said Lottie. "We need lots more marks. When the other animals learn about our letter, they'll all want to sign it too."

And they did.

There were **TOOTH-MARKS** from a lion

and **HOOF-MARKS** from a giraffe

and more **PAW-MARKS,** from a bear

and **CLAW-MARKS** from a parrot

and **WING-MARKS**

and **STING-MARKS**

and **LEG-MARKS**

and **EGG-MARKS**

and **SCALE-MARKS**

and **TAIL-MARKS**

and **TOOTH-MARKS**

and **HOOF-MARKS**

"Now the letter's finished," said Lottie.
"Shall we post it?" said Max.
"No," said Lottie, "we'll march with it."

Lottie and Max marched in front, and behind them came all the creatures who had put their marks on Lottie's letter.

The procession went on till it came to the Chair in the Air, where the Queen of the World sat, floating.
She said: "WISE! WONDERFUL! WELL DONE!
I have never seen a letter with so many paw-marks, claw-marks, wing-marks, sting-marks, leg-marks, egg-marks, scale-marks, tail-marks, tooth-marks and hoof-marks."

THE WORLD IS PRECIOUS, EVERY BIT-
PLEASE DON'T MAKE A MESS OF IT!

Lottie
max

"What will you do?" asked Lottie.
"I shall fly round the world with the letter," said the Queen, "and tell everyone to stop making such a muck and a muddle and a mess. Otherwise, the world may come to an end, and what will become of us all then?"

Lottie and Max gazed up as the Queen
flew away to warn the people, calling out:

"THE WORLD IS PRECIOUS, EVERY BIT -
PLEASE DON'T MAKE A MESS OF IT!"

"I hope the people will listen," said Lottie.
And so do we all.